WELCOM
PASSPORT TO ~~READING~~

A beginning reader's ticket to a brand-new world!

Every book in this program is designed to build read-along and read-alone skills, level by level, through engaging and enriching stories. As the reader turns each page, he or she will become more confident with new vocabulary, sight words, and comprehension.

These PASSPORT TO READING levels will help you choose the perfect book for every reader.

READING TOGETHER
Read short words in simple sentence structures together to begin a reader's journey.

READING OUT LOUD
Encourage developing readers to sound out words in more complex stories with simple vocabulary.

READING INDEPENDENTLY
Newly independent readers gain confidence reading more complex sentences with higher word counts.

READY TO READ MORE
Readers prepare for chapter books with fewer illustrations and longer paragraphs.

This book features sight words from the educator-supported Dolch Sight Words List. This encourages the reader to recognize commonly used vocabulary words, increasing reading speed and fluency.

For more information, please visit passporttoreadingbooks.com.

Enjoy the journey!

HASBRO and its logo, MY LITTLE PONY and all related characters are trademarks of Hasbro and are used with permission. © 2017 Hasbro. All Rights Reserved. MY LITTLE PONY: THE MOVIE © 2017 My Little Pony Productions, LLC.

Cover design by Elaine Levine.

Hachette Book Group supports the right to free expression and the value of copyright. The purpose of copyright is to encourage writers and artists to produce the creative works that enrich our culture.

The scanning, uploading, and distribution of this book without permission is a theft of the author's intellectual property. If you would like permission to use material from the book (other than for review purposes), please contact permissions@hbgusa.com. Thank you for your support of the author's rights.

Little, Brown and Company
Hachette Book Group
1290 Avenue of the Americas, New York, NY 10104
Visit us at lb-kids.com
mylittlepony.com

First Edition: August 2017

Little, Brown and Company is a division of Hachette Book Group, Inc. The Little, Brown name and logo are trademarks of Hachette Book Group, Inc. The publisher is not responsible for websites (or their content) that are not owned by the publisher.

Library of Congress Control Number 2017943154

ISBNs: 978-0-316-55755-9 (pbk.), 978-0-316-47878-6 (Scholastic edition), 978-0-316-55756-6 (ebook), 978-0-316-55757-3 (ebook), 978-0-316-55753-5 (ebook)

Printed in the United States of America

CW

10 9 8 7 6 5 4 3 2 1

Passport to Reading titles are leveled by independent reviewers applying the standards developed by Irene Fountas and Gay Su Pinnell in *Matching Books to Readers: Using Leveled Books in Guided Reading*, Heinemann, 1999.

Licensed By:

Friends and Foes

Adapted by Magnolia Belle

Based on the Screenplay by

Meghan McCarthy and Rita Hsiao

Produced by Brian Goldner and Stephen Davis

Directed by Jayson Thiessen

LITTLE, BROWN AND COMPANY
New York   Boston

Attention, My Little Pony fans!
Look for these words when you read
this book. Can you spot them all?

tea

Sonic
Rainboom

whirlpool

cake

Everypony is so excited for the
Friendship Festival!
Equestria's biggest star,
Songbird Serenade,
will sing for all Canterlot!

An angry Unicorn named
Tempest Shadow brings a storm
to the party.
"I work for the Storm King.
Give your magic to him."
Princesses Celestia, Luna,
and Cadance refuse.
Tempest turns them to stone!

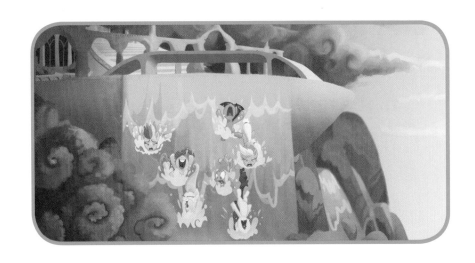

Princess Twilight Sparkle escapes.
"We have to get help!" she says.

Twilight Sparkle and her friends
go to a strange town where
they meet a cat.

His name is Capper.

Capper invites the ponies to his house.
He makes them tea.

Tempest tracks the ponies
to Capper's house!
They sneak out and get away.

They escape to a flying pirate ship!

The captain is named Celaeno.

She is very strong and fun.

Rainbow Dash is excited about
her new pirate friends.
She makes a Sonic Rainboom.
Tempest sees it in the sky.

She goes to the ship.
The ponies escape!

Twilight Sparkle uses magic
to make a hot-air balloon!

The ponies fly it to Mount Aris.

The city is empty.

"Where is everypony?" Twilight asks.

Soon, they see a strange creature swimming.

It gets scared and goes underwater. The ponies dive after the creature. They get caught in a whirlpool!

The ponies are now in Seaquestria.
They even make a new friend
named Princess Skystar.
She is a Seapony.

Princess Skystar takes the ponies
to meet her mom.
Her name is Queen Novo.
Princess Twilight Sparkle tells
Queen Novo about Tempest
and the Storm King.

Queen Novo shows the ponies
a magical pearl.

Queen Novo uses the pearl's magic
to change her new pony friends
into Seaponies.
Spike is a puffer fish!
They love it and swim all over!

Princess Skystar also introduces
the ponies to Shelly and Sheldon.
They are her seashell friends!

The ponies decide to have a
party for Princess Skystar.

Pinkie Pie sings a song about friendship!
Queen Novo loves Pinkie Pie's message!

It is time for the ponies to go home
and face the Storm King.
Queen Novo turns them all back
into ponies.

When nopony is looking,
Tempest catches Twilight!

Twilight's friends do not know what to do.
Just then, their new friends arrive
to help save the day!

Meanwhile, Tempest tells Twilight how
she is sad about her broken horn.
Twilight Sparkle says, "Tempest,
I am the Princess of Friendship.
I want to help you."

Twilight Sparkle's new friends
hide inside a giant cake and
say it is for the Storm King.

They jump out of it and surprise him!

The Storm King is angry and
uses his magic staff
to make a giant tornado!
Tempest almost
gets sucked into it.
Twilight Sparkle
saves her!

Twilight Sparkle sends the Storm King
back into his own storm!

Everypony cheers!

Princess Twilight Sparkle uses the
magic staff to save the Princesses Celestia,
Luna, and Cadance.

Tempest is so grateful to have
new friends.
She tells them her real name
is Fizzlepop Berrytwist,
and she uses her broken horn
to make fireworks in the sky!